Mara L. Pratt-Chadwick

Francisco Pizarro

the conquest of Peru

Mara L. Pratt-Chadwick

Francisco Pizarro
the conquest of Peru

ISBN/EAN: 9783337383282

Printed in Europe, USA, Canada, Australia, Japan

Cover: Foto ©Andreas Hilbeck / pixelio.de

More available books at **www.hansebooks.com**

FOLKS' LIBRARY OF AMERICAN HISTORY.

RANCISCO PIZARRO.

THE
CONQUEST OF PERU.

BY MARA L. PRATT, M. D.

OR OF " AMERICAN HISTORY STORIES."—" CORTES AND
"FAIRYLAND OF FLOWERS," ETC., ETC.

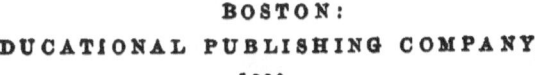

BOSTON:
EDUCATIONAL PUBLISHING COMPANY,
1890.

FRANCISCO PIZARRO.

YOUNG FOLKS' LIBRARY OF AMERICAN HISTORY.

Francisco Pizarro.

I suppose it would be hardly fair to our boy readers to keep from them the story of Pizarro's "running away," — much as there is to be said against filling the heads of lads with stories of that kind. But, you see, Pizarro was a boy of rather unusual type, and the times, too, four hundred years ago, were very different from those of to-day. The New World had just been discovered; European countries were at war with each other; ships were only just beginning to be built strong enough to sail far out to sea; and navigation, adventure, exploration, and discovery were the watchwords of the hour.

5

Pizarro's father, who was a soldier full of daring, but of very little moral worth, seems to have bequeathed his son nothing but his name and his bold spirit. Pizarro's mother, a low peasant woman, had no choice in the matter, even had she wished to see her boy brought up in the poor way common to children of her caste.

Almost as soon as he could walk, this black-eyed, fiery-hearted little Spaniard was set to work watching the herds of pigs as they wallowed and grunted about — just as pigs do to-day, except that those were given the liberty of the roads and mires, and any other place where the filth and garbage were sufficient to give their pig-ships pleasure.

This was the life Pizarro led until, when fifteen years old, his ambitious spirit could endure it no longer. Poor little fellow! He had known little of the joys of childhood. All these years he had grown up amid those mean, squalid surroundings, ignorance and filth and poverty his only education, watching the pigs from dawn till dark, eating only the coarsest food, sleeping at night on a bed of dirty hay, and with all this, beaten and kicked for the slightest neglect of his duties.

Such a life as this would kill out the fire and ambition of

any boy, and make him into an animal as stupid and brutish as those Pizarro watched.

SPANISH PEASANTS.

But Pizarro had inherited from his father so fierce and proud a spirit, that even this grovelling life could not kill it. It seemed rather to increase it — this daily wretchedness and tyranny ; and, as he came up into his "teens," he chafed angrily at his revolting labor and his brutal masters.

It happened one day as he was about his work, his blood

boiling and his heart beating angrily over some fresh injustice from his master, that a sailor arrived in the little village, bringing with him wonderful stories of the "new land" across the sea. "Oh, such a wonderful land!" the sailor said. "Gold, silver and precious stones! A land of plenty!" In his rough way the sailor went on to tell about the voyage; the excitement of the landing; the wonderful explorations; the strange, copper-colored people, and, above all, the number of ships that were already being built in the different Spanish sea-ports to go out again across the great sea to this wonderful new land.

The little swineherd was fired with ambition to see this new land. All the pent-up passion of his life burst forth; all the longings, dreamings, all his schemes for future greatness went rushing through his brain at red-hot speed.

Here, indeed, was a career worthy of his courage and ambition. "I shall go!" cried Pizarro. "I shall go!"

From that day Pizarro had but one plan — to escape, make his way to Seville, join the army, and some time go to the wonderful land of which the sailor had told him.

Among the many swineherds were two boys of Pizarro's

PIZARRO AND COMPANIONS ON FOOT FOR SEVILLE.

own age, in whom he had found no little sympathy in days
gone by, when, from time to time, he had burst into indig-
nant fury at their wretched lives among the pigs. To
these two boys Pizarro unfolded his new plans and his
scheme for escape. Readily the boys fell in with their
leader, and all three joined in preparation for the time when
escape would be possible.

An opportunity came at last; and in the dead of the
night, the three boys, each with a little bundle thrown over
his shoulder, in which were food and all their worldly
possessions, crept out from the village up the mountain
road.

It was just at daybreak when they reached the summit of
a rough, steep cliff, from which they could look down upon
the village.

"Just see how small the village looks!" cried one of the
boys. "We must have climbed a long distance to have it
look so far away."

"We're done with Truxillo, thank heaven!" exclaimed
Francisco, throwing himself down to rest on the broad
cliff. "No more watching swine for us! We will be soldiers or sailors, and we'll cross the sea, and fight our way to
fame and glory!"

"But it is a long journey to Seville," said the youngest
of the three boys. "How shall we ever reach there?"

"What, Pedro, are you afraid? Away with such coward-
words! I'd rather starve than go back to that slave's
work! Come, come! Courage, Pedro, courage!"

THE BOYS ARRIVE IN SEVILLE.

It was a long, hard journey that lay before these desperate
boys. Over hills, along hot, dusty roads, across streams,
and over parched and barren fields they tramped bravely
on, resting one night beneath the warm shelter of some
good peasant's roof, another by the roadside or beneath
some forest trees.

But the lads had youth and health and courage, and, best
of all, an honest, steady purpose to help them on their
way. And one bright, warm evening, just as the setting
sun was gilding the clouds and reflecting its sunset glory
upon the towers and domes of the beautiful city, our travel-
worn lads came within the gates of Seville.

"Was ever anything so grand?" exclaimed Pizarro, as

the grand steeple of the great cathedral and the great towers of the Alcazar rose high before them.

THE GIRALDA, SEVILLE.

Their arrival seemed indeed well timed. Soldiers, soldiers, appeared on every side. Amidst the crowds of people, hurrying along the street, in the windows of the balconied dwellings, in the gardens, in the cathedral — everywhere glittered and shone the beautiful armor of the Spanish soldiers.

All this but rekindled the fire in Pizarro's heart. To be a soldier, to wear an armor like that, to fight, to win fame! such were the ambitions of Pizarro. Though but fifteen, he was tall, straight and strong, brave, daring and resolute. "Sir," said Pizarro, walking boldly up to an officer, "we three lads have run away from home to join the army. We are ready to go anywhere or do anything, and we want to join at once."

The officer, recognizing at once that in these boys were that fire and daring of which soldiers are made, took them to the captain, and they were at once enrolled as soldiers in the Spanish army, pledged to fight for Ferdinand and Isabella against the French.

Now the three lads separated; and Pizarro, with whom we have — in this story especially — to do, dressed in the showy uniform of his time, began his life as a soldier.

On reaching Italy, where the war against the French usurper was carried on, Pizarro was able only to take part in the final battles. But such was his bravery, his strength,

the fire with which he fought, the resolute patience with
which he endured the hardship of the march and the camp,

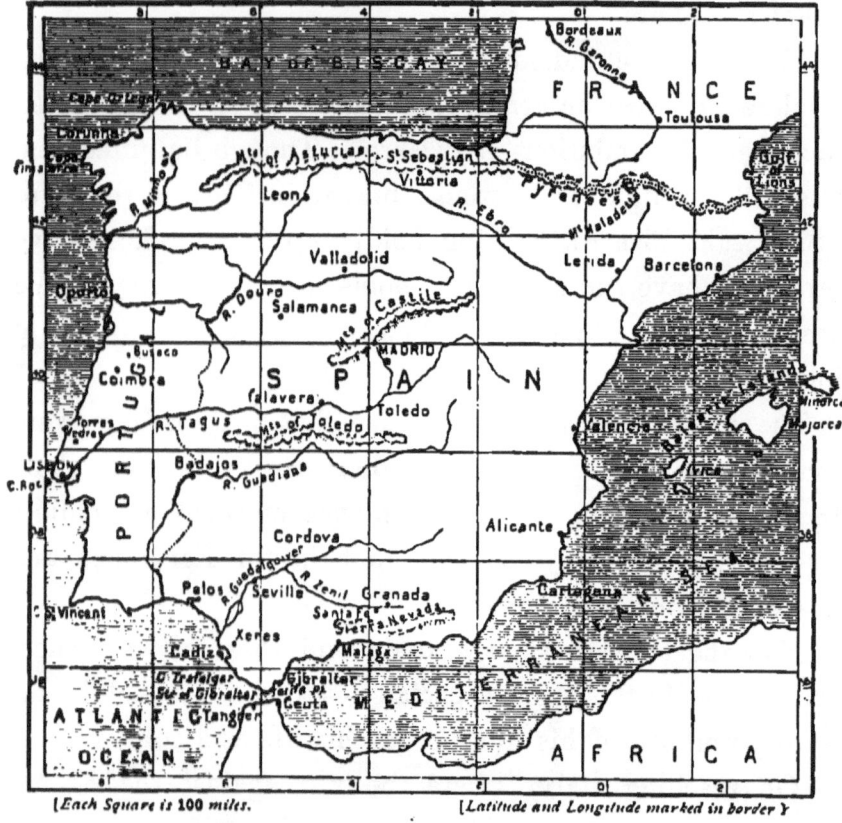

[Each Square is 100 miles. [Latitude and Longitude marked in border ?

that, in this short time even, he had won the good-will of
his officers and the respect of his fellow soldiers.

On his return to Seville, as reward for his valor he was made lieutenant; and as he marched about the city in his beautiful, glittering uniform, I hardly think, except in the same eager eye and manly bearing, you would have recognized him as the dusty, ragged swineherd of a few months before.

For several years he served in the army, gaining every year new honors and higher rank; and had army life been always on the field, doubtless even his restless spirit would have found ample scope in such a career; but there were the long intervening months of barrack life — stupid, intolerable months of imprisonment, so they seemed to Pizarro.

Again the old fever and ambition to win wealth and fame in the New World burned within him. A life of bold adventure, of continual conflict, even perpetual danger, was Pizarro's only dream of happiness.

Every day, as reports of this wonderful New World came to his ears, he grew more and more restless and determined. Such opportunities for conquest, wealth, power, fame!

Already Spain was ringing with the reports of the enormous wealth, the vast lands, the beautiful climate, the

strange, copper-colored people of the New World. And
when at last an expedition was fitted out, whose commander
called for brave, hardy men with military experience, men
who were strong and daring, ready to brave the hardships
of the rude forest life, Pizarro hastened to join the party, to
offer his sword and his genius to the new expedition to the
New World.

PIZARRO IN AMERICA.

We can no longer think of Pizarro as the enthusiastic,
daring soldier-boy. Many years have passed since he so
boldly presented himself to the Spanish officer and enrolled
himself with the king's soldiers.

He is now a full-grown man, hardened by the rigid military life, his body and mind both strengthened by contact
with the rough experiences of a rough life. Perhaps Pizarro
was a hero ; no doubt his courage and his ambition were
commendable ; and we would not filch from him one word
of the praise and admiration which belong to him. Still

we cannot but be glad that such ruthless, defiant, selfish characters as the adventurer are not in this day needed to sustain our civilization and to promote our progress. We are glad that, in this day, the self-made man knows that to be truly honored and respected, to be of real help and value to his fellow-men, he must not, in his struggle for self-elevation, allow himself to grow so selfish and hardened as to lose all the finer, gentler, nobler qualities of manhood.

Physical courage in Pizarro's day, boys, was no doubt in the minds of the people, the grandest thing; but in these days, the world expects something better than that of its heroes. Men like Cortes and Pizarro are well to read about—we need to read about them in fact; but don't take them for your models. Remember that the world's heroes to-day must not only be brave, ambitious, progressive, but they must withal be *gentle-men*.

Brevity is the soul of wit, they say; yes, and it's the very pith of a sermon, isn't it? So let us go back again to Pizarro, who, if he isn't to-day, was, at least, then, in the fifteenth and sixteenth centuries, the type of a "great hero."

Amid sturdy men like himself, filled with the same fire
of cupidity and thirst for fame and conquest, Pizarro entered
heart and soul into the schemes laid before him during the
long voyage.   Conscious that he himself was able to command, he determined to lose no opportunity for pushing
himself into such positions as would better his fortunes.

FIGHT WITH THE INDIANS.

On reaching the New World, he was at once taken into
the confidence of Alonzo de Ojeda, one of the boldest and
fiercest of the Spanish adventurers there — a man who was
famous already for the daring with which he assailed the
natives, and the pitiless way in which he destroyed them,
broke up their families, and sold them into slavery.

Now, Ojeda had been made governor of a part of the
Isthmus of Darien, and was sadly in need of another, as
daring as himself, to go there and overcome the native
Indian.   Pizarro, according to Ojeda's judgment, was just
the man for the occasion ; and the occasion, according to
Pizarro's judgment, was just the one for Pizarro.

Although warned of the hostility of the natives, Pizarro and Ojeda set forth in excellent spirits for the Isthmus. They were indeed a well-mated pair of officers, fear being as much a stranger to the one as to the other.

But for all that, the expedition was doomed to fail. No sooner had their ship's keels grated upon the shore than down from the hills and out from the forests swarmed the natives, armed with their deadly, poisoned arrows.

In an hour seventy Spaniards lay dead upon the shore ; and the rest, many of them already writhing in the agony of death from their poison wounds, were driven back to their ships. Ojeda himself, cutting his way through the infuriated savages, escaped half-dead to the forest. There he was found the following day, and carried, fainting, to his vessel.

But Ojeda was not the man to die or to be discouraged by one defeat. Calling Pizarro to him as soon as he was able to speak, he gave the colony into his charge, and made arrangements to go back to Hispaniola, from whence they had come, for help.

For fifty long weary days did Pizarro and his companions wait for Ojeda's return. And now, so few of the men

PIZARRO'S FIGHT WITH THE INDIANS.

lived, that their one ship could carry them all ; and Pizarro set sail from the wretched place for Hispaniola.

Pizarro Joins Balboa.

In no wise discouraged, however, Pizarro at once joined the forces of Balboa, the governor-general of this same Isthmus. Balboa had been told by friendly Indians that beyond the Isthmus was a great and mighty ocean,—as great and as broad as the Atlantic. If this was true, Balboa was determined to be the first to gaze upon the undiscovered waters. So, getting together a band of his strongest and sturdiest men, and taking with him a herd of cruel bloodhounds, Balboa, with Pizarro as his lieutenant, set out again for the Isthmus of Darien.

There were danger and glory both in this expedition, and in both Pizarro had his share. A friendly chief, Ponca, accompanied Balboa as guide. Coming out from the dense forest one morning, Ponca cried, "There ! there ! from that mountain you can see the great ocean rolling at your feet ! "

Although yet far distant, Balboa pushed eagerly onward. But they were now in the country of hostile Indians. Down came the tribes, showering upon the white men their arrows, and attacking them with spears and clubs.

"Fire upon them!" was Pizarro's command. Instantly out blazed the fire and smoke, the echo thundering on and on from mountain to mountain. The Indians, having never heard a gun-report, ran shrieking and howling back to their village. The Spaniards pursued, and no less than six hundred of them fell dead. The few who escaped fled to the mountain, and Balboa and his men were free to enter their village and plunder to their heart's content. Much food was found stored away in the huts of the village; and what was almost dearer still to the Spanish adventurer's soul, gold and silver and precious stones.

Leaving a number of his men to guard the store, Balboa pushed on to the mountain. It was at daybreak, one bright September morning, in 1513, that the foot of the mountain was reached.

"This is the peak," repeated Ponca, "from which you can see our great ocean."

First View of the Ocean.

Balboa's heart beat with excitement. "If this is true," said he in his ambitious mind, "I shall be a discoverer — a discoverer! — and I shall be famous throughout all Europe."

"My good men," said he, turning to his followers, "rest you here. I alone will climb to the summit. Mine shall be the eyes first to behold this wonderful ocean that glistens on the other side of this great wall."

Then, springing up the mountain side, and from cliff to cliff, he made his way to the summit. His followers watched eagerly from below.

There, in truth, lay spread out before him, the boundless waters of the ocean. Balboa was indeed a discoverer! He would indeed be honored by the European nations!

Eagerly signalling to his men to follow him, he sank down upon the mountain top, overcome by the beauty of the scene before him and his own contending thoughts.

Such beauty! such breadth! such peace! Such a picture had never entered the vision of Balboa even in his wildest dreams. And now, descending upon the ocean side, they explored the shore along the Isthmus, collected a goodly amount of treasure, and returned in safety to the colony.

During the absence of Balboa, a new governor had been sent over to take the charge of Darien. Balboa might well have resisted this injustice, but gallant cavalier that he was, he welcomed him with all honor.

It is a pity the new governor was not more deserving of this generous treatment from Balboa. But as was too often the case among these adventurers, personal interests and the gratification of selfish ambitions overruled; and, after having gleaned from Balboa all the information necessary to carry on the exploration of the coast of the new ocean, this new governor ordered that Balboa be set aside, and if he made trouble, that he be arrested and thrown into prison.

Pizarro Heads an Expedition.

The new governor then fitted out an expedition in his own name, putting Pizarro at the head of it. It was an expedition fatal to many a brave Spaniard; for on reaching the Pacific coast, Pizarro divided his forces, and with one part set off for a group of islands, on whose shores he had been told were pearls without number. No sooner had the Spaniards landed than the natives, convinced that they came on no friendly visit, fell upon them in true Indian fashion. A long, hard battle followed, and it was only after great loss that the Spaniards were able to get possession of the island. As reward for all this loss of life, Pizarro found a vast number of very large and brilliant pearls, and also a large quantity of gold ; enough, one would think, to satisfy even the most grasping and ambitious man.

When the new governor saw all these golden signs of wealth, he immediately resolved to cross the Isthmus to the point now called Panama, and there, on the Pacific coast, build the palace of the future capital.

Pizarro accompanied the governor to the new site for the capital city. There, having now gained wealth and fame, he laid out for himself a fine estate, as we should call it in these days, was served by a retinue of Indian servants, and was held in high respect as one of the cavaliers who had had his part in the conquering and settling of this great country.

Cities of Gold.

Pizarro was now more than forty years of age, and except we remember that discovery and exploration were the watchwords of the time, we should almost think he would be "a-weary" of his life, so full of hardship and of strife, and would be glad indeed to live, for a while at least, a quiet life, surrounded by ease and comfort.

But selfish as Pizarro was, his selfishness happened not to find its fulness in this manner of living.

His bold adventurous spirit longed rather for the stirring excitement of the battle-field, and the perils of exploration. Day after day, as he looked over his broad and beautiful fields, he saw no beauty in their quiet, and no comfort in their possession. According to his estimate of what a successful life should be, of what a hero is, he was but in the swine-herd days again

What to him were wealth and comfort compared with the fame of his first gallant chief, Balboa! what compared with the world-renowned conquests of Cortes!

Well, there's the old saying that "where there's a will there's a way." Pizarro certainly had will enough, and so it came about, I presume, that one day there came into port an explorer who had been far down the Pacific coast.

"There," said he, "are natives very different from these savages of Darien.   There are cities there, and gold and precious stones."

It was the same old, old story that had urged on every Spaniard since the discovery of the New World ; the old, old story that had excited their cupidity, urged them on in their cruelty, and driven them to their death.

Pizarro's ambition blazed up anew.   Already he saw in eager anticipation the city that, like Mexico, he should overcome.   Pizarro and Cortes ! Cortes and Pizarro !

Fortunately for Pizarro, others in the colony had been fired by the explorer's story of gold, and all were ready together to fit out a fleet.   Pizarro was put in command, and a force of a hundred brave, sturdy men was gathered together.

With this little force, Pizarro set forth upon his journey to an undiscovered country, knowing little more than that glory or death — as likely one as the other — awaited them all.

Like Columbus or Cortes, he set forth, his heart bursting with hope and ambition; and like them, too, he had before him a conquest, of the greatness of which, in his wildest flights, he had never dreamed.

The Land of the Inca.

While Pizarro is on his way, let us take a flight in mind to this mysterious land to which our hero is to come.

It is, indeed, a marvellous country. More marvellous than even the explorer who had told Pizarro of it had imagined. Nearing the shore, one would hardly be attracted to the country, and would hardly dream of the wonders beyond the mountains. It doesn't seem as if the soil were worthy of cultivation even, so barren and craggy do the mountains look. But let us go nearer. Wonders upon wonders! What manner of people are here, pray, that they build bridges and canals and aqueducts? And see! the sides of the mountains, which from the ocean looked so barren, are covered with gardens, terraced one above the other, to the very tops. And there are houses, too, upon these terraces. Upon the mountain sides

browse herds of long-haired sheep — llamas we call them
now;

LLAMA.

and upon the high table-lands on the tops of the mountains are other towns and villages, with their long, straight
roads, their thrifty dwellings, and their luxuriant gardens.

This is Peru, the land of the Inca, as the Peruvians
called their ruler.

How They Lived.

The Peruvians, we may as well learn here, were Sun-worshippers. The Sun, they believed, in order that his chosen people, the Peruvians, might be prosperous, had sent his only son and his only daughter to live among them, and to teach them such arts as would give them riches and power.

The brother founded his capital at Cuzco, and then taught the Peruvians how to cultivate their farms and gardens, to supply themselves with water, to build canals, bridges and houses. Then the sister came; she took the women under her instruction, teaching them to weave, to spin, and to cook.

So it was that the empire of Peru was founded by the children of the Sun; and when this brother and sister had gone away, the son's children had been given charge over the people, and the realm had ever since passed down from one generation to another of these children of the Sun — the Incas.

All high places in church or state or battle-field were held by the members of the families descended from the Sun.

In regard to that Inca who was to become the next
monarch, these rude people had certain established conditions, from which many a modern monarchy might well
learn useful lessons. He was obliged to pass a life of
study, to be skilled in military affairs, learned in the history of his people, and, before taking his throne, to prove
in severe examinations his ability to rule intelligently over
his people.

When, however, the Inca was made king, then his word
was absolute, his will divine law. Standing, as he now
did, as the representative of the Sun, he was an object
of worship. Even the Inca nobles could now appear
before him only with bared feet and uncovered head,
carrying upon their backs a burden in token of their
acknowledged inferiority.

The monarch was the high-priest also; and in this
double office ruled both church and state. Such beautiful
palaces of silver and gold, studded with sparkling gems,
as the Incas had! Even the glories of the Montezumas
paled before them! And their temple! Great bars of
gold for cornices, rods of shining silver for the altars, and
the walls covered from floor to ceiling with golden plates
and ornaments!

RUINS OF REPUTED TEMPLE OF THE SUN AT PACHA-CAMAC.

The Inca was never tyrannical, though perfect obedience was demanded. The farms were re-divided every year, and the people were thus never allowed to grow rich, neither were they ever poor. Each farmer did a share of the tilling of the farms of the nobility, then he performed a certain amount of labor upon those lands dedicated to the Sun, besides which he must do his share towards cultivating the farms of the sick and aged — the rest of his time was his own.

Every trade, every art was, in a similar way, controlled by a central government ; and whether wise or not, this form of control certainly had the effect of producing the greatest harmony between rulers and people, success in all arts and trades, prosperity in their nation, and power over their enemies

Such was the beautiful land of the Incas. Such was the peaceful, law-abiding people upon whom Pizarro was so soon to descend. Such the quiet, prosperous nation, so soon to lie a noble ruin at Pizarro's feet.

PIZARRO'S JOURNEY.

Pizarro was brave and daring. Fear was no more known to his nature now than it had been in his boyhood. Still, with only a hundred men, journeying through a rough, unknown country, inhabited by hostile Indians, what could even the bravest commander hope to gain? Had the jealous governor, the same one who had so unjustly overthrown Balboa, given Pizarro a fleet of any size, and forces of any number worthy of such an undertaking, Pizarro would have been sure of success.

With even his few men, Pizarro pushed his way southward nearly to Peru. On the journey he fought desperately with hostile tribes along the shore, often driving them back into the forests, frightened and subdued. A large amount of gold was thus collected, and many precious stones. But in all these battles Spaniards fell, until at last Pizarro, knowing that to push on was worse than useless, embarked his few remaining men, and turned his vessel homeward. Landing on an island not far from Darien, he sent his treasure to the governor by a fellow-voyager, with the request that a larger fleet be fitted out, and that a force be given him sufficiently large to conquer the people in this southern gold country.

Again the governor was seized with jealousy as he viewed the golden treasure and heard the wonderful reports about those southern Indians. But Luque, a priest, asserting his authority as church official, compelled the governor to do as he should. Funds were procured, ships built, and again Pizarro started forth, — this time with Almagro, his faithful friend.

Together they sailed directly to the farthest point along the coast which had, in a previous voyage, been reached by

Almagro. Reconnoitering here, Pizarro was convinced that they were upon the border-lands of hostile, warlike tribes. Surely more men would be needed. Accordingly Almagro returned to Panama, while Pizarro and his few men held their position until he should return. It was a long and dreary waiting. Sickness, starvation, treachery surrounded them on every side. No wonder the bravest of them loudly bewailed their wretched plight, and regretted bitterly the folly that had led them from comfortable homes to such a land as this.

Here, as ever in times of sore distress, Pizarro proved the heroism of his character. Sharing his last mouthful with his men, working with them and for them, by his courage and patience and ready sympathy, he kept them from despair, until at last, when hope seemed almost dead, Ruiz, who had been sent to coast along the shore, appeared in sight.

With food and gold, and with a thrilling story of the prospects farther south, Ruiz revived the ambition in these half-dead men, and soon no word was heard other than that expressing willingness, yes, even impatience to go on to the wonderful lands farther south.

Almagro soon returned from Panama, bringing with him some eighty men, all eager for adventure. A new governor had been installed during their voyage, and welcome news it was indeed to Almagro and Pizarro.

A Second Attempt.

Now, all miseries and discontent forgotten, spirits revived by the arrival of food and clothes as well as by the courage and eagerness of the eighty new arrivals,— all set forth again down the Pacific coast.

It seemed now as if Pizarro deserved success ; that is, if such a cruel errand as that upon which he had set forth could be said to merit favor. Surely he had proved himself no coward, and had bravely held his own in time of trial.

For a few days all seemed prosperous. Then arose a gale of wind — such, Pizarro said, as had never been known on Atlantic waters. Then storms burst upon them, and for a time it seemed as if the brave sailors had escaped famine and massacre only to be now destroyed by the tempest.

Putting into St. Matthew's Bay, they were sheltered until the storm had passed.

Then, on again they sped, rejoicing in the bright, sparkling waters, and in the increasing signs of thrift along the shore.

One morning, as they were skimming along, full of hope and eagerly watching each bend in the coast, Pizarro called, "Almagro! Almagro! see this village! It has houses!"

"And streets!" cried Almagro, alive in an instant.

"And look, the people glitter with golden ornaments!"

The natives on board told them this was one of the famous towns of their land; and, what appealed far more than its beauty or its fame to the Spaniards, that the pretty river winding through the town was full of large and rare emeralds.

"Let us land!" said the impetuous Pizarro.

"Let us land!" echoed the greedy sailors. And so busy were they with the hurried preparations for landing, and so filled were their minds with visions of great, green emeralds.

with which they would load themselves and their ships, that they hardly saw the rush of the natives to the shore until the javelins whizzed about their ears.

Their situation was now one of peril. What but quick work on the part of every sailor-could save them!

"To the ship! to the ship!" called the commander. "To the ship! to the ship!" shouted the sailors. Then followed a rush for life! Everyone flew to his place! Escape seemed hopeless! Already the Indians were at the water's edge! Canoes were darting out from every nook! It was indeed a moment of excitement. Almagro and Pizarro seemed everywhere. "For your lives, my men! For your lives!"

THEY ARE SAVED.

And what do you suppose saved them? No flash of lightning from a clear sky, as the novels have it; no sudden eclipse of the sun. No supernatural uprising of old Neptune. Simply this — one soldier in his hurry and

flurry lost his balance and fell from his horse. Imagine the
surprise of the fallen soldier and all the rest,when the natives,
instead of seizing upon him, dropped their bows, gave one
howl, and fled up the mountain.

"What is it?" cried Pizarro, pausing in his work.

"They thought the horse and the rider were one animal,"
said the native captives, gloomily · "and they were frightened to see it separate itself."

A loud laugh went up from the rescued band, and they
lost no time in getting themselves on board, and in
readiness to leave these inhospitable shores.

ALMAGRO GOES BACK TO PANAMA.

"It is fool-hardiness," said Pizarro, as they sailed away,
"to attempt to attack such swarms of savages as there
seem to be along this shore, with such a little company as
this. I will go back to Panama for help.

"You will not," said Almagro angrily. "I myself will go."

"You're a coward!" shouted Pizarro. "You dare not

face the possible misery of famine while waiting for more men. You would have me always stay while you choose the far easier part of going to the land of plenty. I say it is this time my *right* to go."

A bitter quarrel ensued. How it ended matters little. Enough for us just here to know that Almagro carried the point and went to Panama.

When the sailors learned that they were again to be left to the mercies of this strange land and still stranger people, they rebelled. It was of no avail, however; and when they found escape impossible, they wrote letters to their friends in Panama, telling them a pitiful story of suffering and ill-treatment. These letters they concealed in bales of cotton which Almagro was to carry to Panama.

These letters when found were taken to the governor, and appeal made to him for the rescue of these men. The governor, exasperated at the story these letters told, sternly rebuked Almagro for concealing from him the truth. "Not only will I send no more aid," said he, "but I will at once dispatch a ship to bring Pizarro and the ill-used men back to Panama."

Nothing Almagro could say would change the decree;

and accordingly when the Spanish vessel appeared off the coast where Pizarro awaited it, it was not to bring the longed-for aid, but to bring an order from the governor that to Pizarro was more bitter than death.

When the ship's commander delivered the governor's order, the men were wild with delight. And if you could have seen them, — sick, starving, their clothes in tatters, drenched with rain and covered with mud — you would not have blamed them.

PIZARRO'S BRAVE BAND.

Pizarro was determined not to go back to Panama. "It would mean defeat — disgrace! I will not go back like a wounded dog to confess myself a failure. I know that below here is a land of riches. I will *not* turn back with wealth and conquest at my right hand!" Then, striding into the midst of his men, he said, "Comrades, you have now a great question to decide. We stand here where two roads meet. One is full of peril and privation, hard labor,

THE DIVIDING LINE.

storms, famine, the poisoned arrow, the midnight attack of
angry savages; but that road leads to Peru.   Peru! with
its untold wealth, and the endless glory of its conquest.

The other road leads home — to Panama, with its plenty,
its ease and indolence; where you will be clothed and fed,
mayhap, but where contempt will greet you, poverty and
obscurity.   Now choose your way.   For my part, I remain."   Then, drawing a deep line upon the sand, he said,
stepping over on the southern side, " Those of you who will
return to Panama, stay where you are; but you brave men
who dare stand by your captain, who dare share his dangers
and his hardships, his honors and triumphs, follow me and
cross this line."

For a moment, perfect silence.   The men glanced at each
other, some hung their heads, others crept away to the rear.
Then one stepped over, then another, and another.   Thirteen
in all.   A small band you will say to attempt to conquer a
country.   But Pizarro knew Almagro would hear the story
and would lose no time in sending provisions, and perhaps,
soldiers.

For seven long months these fourteen men waited and
watched for help.   Sickness, starvation, insects, poisonous

reptiles, everything of horror that the country could bring forth seemed added to their desolation.

At last a vessel came in sight. With what eagerness the men rushed to the shore! with what desperation they signalled! Fortunately the crew was watching for them. The prow was turned shoreward; the men waded out and climbed up the vessel's sides.

It was indeed a vessel sent by Almagro; but there were no soldiers on it, for the governor, though willing that provisions should be sent these foolhardy men as they seemed to him, still opposed firmly the sacrifice of more men.

Pizarro was disappointed indeed. But he was not the man to sulk or to refuse such aid as the vessel had brought. The provisions at least were acceptable as the half starved men soon proved. And it was worth something to get even a little fresh powder for their guns.

Pizarro had no idea of returning in the vessel to Panama. " We'll die here rather than go back there to be jeered at," said he, and his brave men were of the same mind. So the good vessel, instead of carrying them home, bore them farther south, nearer the land of gold — the land which some day Pizarro was sure he should conquer.

THE CITY OF TUMBEZ.

It was a daring deed, no doubt, for Pizarro to set forth with this one little vessel into a country which was in all probability inhabited by millions of brave warriors. But as he said, death was more bearable by far than the jeers of his country-men. Well he knew that all his daring, all the suffering he had undergone would count nothing with them were he not able to bring proof that a great empire existed at least in South America.

So they sailed on past the Island of Gallo, past Cape St. Helena. At last the Gulf of Guayaquil was reached.

"See! see!" cried the Indian interpreters. "Here is the land of the Incas! See, there is Quito! And there on the coast is the city of Tumbez, and not far away the city of Puna."

Pizarro gazed longingly at this country, which, for the present, he must be content to look upon, gain some information regarding it perhaps, and then sail quietly away.

Pizarro made up his mind to approach Tumbez, and, if possible, land and enter the city.

"Let us enter as friends," said he, "and see to it that we

do no harm and in no wise arouse suspicion in the natives of our real object."

Tumbez was a wonderful place to the eyes of those Spaniards, who had never dreamed of such splendor even in the " land of gold." The strong fortresses up among the crags, the aqueducts, the temples, the palaces, the broad, well-kept streets all filled the Spaniards with wonder and delight. The people, too, dressed in gay colors and glittering bracelets and chains of gold and silver, served to intensify their visions of future conquest and their greedy longing for gold.

Down flocked the natives to the shore, filled with wonder on their part at the great white-winged bird coming up their harbor. Up and down the shore they ran, shouting, calling and waving their hands. A boat load of natives pushed off from the shore, full of curiosity, and eager to be the first to examine the strange creatures.

" Let them come close to our vessel," said Pizarro. " Tell them," said he, " that we come as friends, and ask them to send us provisions. Tell them, too, that we wish to send one of our men ashore to speak with their chief."

THE WELCOME OF THE NATIVES.

The chief, honest himself, and supposing the Spaniards to be honest likewise, sent at once a boat-load of fruit, potatoes, corn, game, and fish, and with it a noble messenger of high rank, who should welcome Pizarro and bear greetings from the chief. This noble was richly dressed, of dignified bearing, and had a handsome, intelligent face. You may be sure Pizarro and his men behaved their very best towards this stranger; allowed him to examine every part of the vessel, regaled him with a tempting dinner, and finally sent him away delighted with the great white-winged bird and the wonderful strangers.

Such an odd little incident occurred the next morning! Pizarro, in return for the courtesy of the chief, or governor, on the preceding day, sent one of his men and a negro who had come with the Spaniards from Panama, to the city with pork and chickens as a gift to the governor. No sooner had Molina and the negro stepped on shore than they were surrounded by a crowd of chattering men and women who stared at them in amazement. They wondered at Molina's fair skin and long brown beard; but still more they

wondered at the negro's black skin. One woman, true to
her instinct for cleaning, twisted her scarf over her finger
and attempted to scrub off the black. This made the negro
throw back his head and laugh. Then the Indians saw his
rows of white ivories and it was their turn to laugh.

Suddenly one of the little fowls, Pizarro had sent, thrust
out his head with a hearty " Cock-a-doodle-do! cock-a-
doodle-do!" The natives were struck dumb. "What does
the little fellow say? What does he say?" asked they,
when they had somewhat recovered from their surprise.

The utmost good humor prevailed now, and it was in the
midst of a crowd of admiring friends that Pizarro's men
made their way to the royal palace.

Here they found a handsome building, surrounded by a
guard. Within dwelt the governor, attended by numberless servants, who served their master in the most respectful
manner. On every side throughout the city were evidences
of wealth and thrift.

Pizarro, delighted with what he heard of the apparent
wealth of the city, sent on the next day another man to
display the wonders of the Spanish arms, as well as to learn
more of those conditions of the city which should, by and

by, in Panama, be of value to him in securing the co-opera-
tion of the governor there.

This man, Candia, entered the city, and boldly marched
up the main street carrying his gun upon his shoulder.

"What is it you carry with you on your shoulder?"
asked the curious people. "Make it speak! Make it
speak!"

And Candia did make it speak. Setting up a board, he
aimed at it and fired. The natives, who had been carefully
watching every movement, and wondering what the board
had to do with the gun, fell upon their knees and shrieked
when they saw the flash and heard the crash of the splin-
tered board.

On Candia's return to the ship, Pizarro, convinced that
the city must indeed be rich and wonderful, sailed on farther south, visiting from time to time the towns along the
coast, and receiving always a generous welcome from the
people.

After a few weeks of pleasant voyaging, Pizarro returned
to Tumbez. Here he left three of his own men, and carried in their places two of the natives. Pizarro was far-
sighted; and he saw that not only would it be of advantage

to present these natives to the Governor of Darien, but that later they would prove of great value as interpreters and guides.

Pizarro and the Governor.

Full of hope, Pizarro now sailed for Panama. First to meet him at the quay stood his faithful friends, Almagro and Luque. Such a story as he had to tell! And how their eyes glistened when they saw the gold and silver trinkets, the rare and beautiful cloths, the sparkling gems, the strange, long-haired sheep, which Pizarro had brought to prove the truth of his story.

"But, Pizarro," said Almagro, "the governor is bitterly opposed to any more exploring. He will give us no aid — perhaps not his consent to go even."

"What can be done?" said Pizarro, not one whit discouraged at such a prospect. "But one thing; and that is to appeal directly to the King of Spain. I will go to him myself!"

So the three friends, Pizarro, Almagro, and Luque delib-
erated well upon the plan ; and at length it was decided that
Pizarro should indeed go to Spain and state the case to the
king, carrying with him the gold and silver he had brought
with him from Peru, and also the natives, who should tell
their story for themselves.

PIZARRO IN SPAIN.

We need not follow Pizarro on his voyage. It was
pretty much like the voyage across the Atlantic to-day,
except that his conveyance was a sailing vessel, and was
so at the mercy of "fair winds and foul" that it was seven
long weeks before the fiery-hearted Pizarro reached the
Spanish coast.

The vessel put in at the port of Seville — the same beautiful Seville which more than twenty-five years before he
had left a mere soldier lad. There stood the very same
glittering spire, there towered the same mountain, over

whose sides he and his boy-companions had so eagerly fled. Strange things had happened since then. Through what successes, defeats, perils and dangers had he not passed! What a difference between his sailing forth from this old Spanish city and his return to it! Long before, his fame had reached the land of his birth. The obscure, ragged little wanderer upon the face of the earth now found himself a hero. His wonderful valor, his brilliant achievements, his explorations, he found were the common topic of conversation. Just as so long ago he had listened, with wide-open eyes and mouth, to the sailor stories of the earlier explorers, so now the boys of Seville were listening to the sailor stories of Pizarro's own exploits.

Hardly had our hero landed when he received an invitation from the King to come into his royal presence and report to him the story of his adventures.

Pizarro was received by his royal highness in a great hall, filled with the nobility of Spain. It was a brilliant array of richly-dressed men and women that met the wanderer's sight as he entered the hall. One face among them all attracted him most. It was a dark, sunburned face, bronzed and toughened by exposure to wind and weather.

It was, indeed, the face of our old friend Cortes, the conqueror of Mexico.

"Come forward," said the king, "and tell us of this wonderful land which lies so far to the south."

We already know the story Pizarro was so eager to tell; and when we think how daring and how enthusiastic this adventurer was, and how strong were the proofs he brought of the truth of his report, it is but natural his words were listened to with eager interest and sympathy. King Charles, it is said, sat spell-bound during the whole story, eagerly drinking in every word. And when Pizarro's attendants brought into the hall the odd-looking Peruvian sheep, the chest of golden ornaments and the richly-woven cloths, the king sprang from his chair with a burst of admiration, saying, "Pizarro, Pizarro! Brave and gallant man! Honorable and worthy subject! Wonderful are your deeds, and beyond compensation are your discoveries. You have opened to Spain a dominion richer than her own. You have no rival but our noble Cortes in the greatness of your gifts to Spain. To you shall be granted the permission and the aid to go again to Peru and do with that country as Cortes has done with Mexico. O noble man!

Daring adventurer! Never can Spain repay her debt of gratitude to you!"

And Charles the Fifth called at once his scribes and drew up papers, giving to Pizarro the authority to proceed in his ambitious scheme as he wished.

While his vessels were being fitted out, he made a journey to his old home — the little village in which he had lived his swine-herd life. His proud, soldier-father had long since died, and his peasant mother had passed away, never knowing of the honors that had attended her son's career. Four great, broad-shouldered brothers, however, greeted him, and proudly entertained him as grandly as, in their humble life, they were able, losing no opportunity to avail themselves of whatever honor and riches their hero-brother was willing to bestow upon them.

Fancy the amazement and chagrin on the part of the governor, when, a few weeks later, Pizarro with his new ships and soldiers sailed into the port at Panama. Pizarro was now the hero of the hour. Those who had sneered now fawned upon him; and those who had feared to aid him now pressed their services upon him.

"Surprising," said Pizarro to his friend Almagro, "how

a king's approval gilds my plans in the eyes of my good friends here. However, let us take advantage of all this good will, fickle as it is, get our forces together, and sail away before this fair wind changes."

And so it was that a little later Pizarro's fleet, amid the cheers of the people and the booming of cannon, sailed out from the bay, southward to the wonderful land of Peru.

PIZARRO'S RETURN TO PERU.

Pizarro was now filled with a desperate determination to make the conquest of the country before him. Now he had authority. Now he had power. Now he had an army, loyal, brave, and filled with devotion to their daring leader.

Having landed at St. Matthew's Bay, Pizarro sent the ships back to Panama for re-enforcements, and at once proceeded into the country. "Why dally," said he, "we have come to take Peru. Here it is. Let us begin at once. And let us show there is no failure for such as we."

The march inland, like any march in an unknown country was hard and full of peril. But all this the Spaniards had expected, and so were prepared for. Many days of marching at last brought them upon a beautiful little village nestled down among the hills along the shores of a shining river

"Now for our first attack!" cried Pizarro. "Without delay, *now*, *at once*, let us rush down upon this village."

Before the peaceful natives could even gather their families together for flight, the Spanish army fell upon them, slaughtering some, driving others to the forests, ransacking and burning their homes.

In these huts the soldiers found not only fruit and food, but quantities of gold and silver, and many beautiful stones.

"See! see!" cried a soldier, bringing forward a beautiful green stone.

"It looks like an emerald!" cried a greedy priest. "Pound it with a stone. If it does not break, it is an emerald."

Of course the green jewel broke beneath the blow, and the ignorant soldier hurried away eager for other plunder, while the tricky old monk carefully concealed in the folds of his robe the precious bits of emerald, the value of which he knew only too well.

The plunder from this village was carefully stored away in the vessels when they returned, and were sent to Panama with most glowing reports of what had already been learned of the wonderful new land.

Pizarro continued his line of march, keeping close to the coast. After long days of hard marching, during which no more villages of plenty appeared upon which to feast themselves, with sickness, and no little discouragement among the men, Pizarro found himself once more on the very frontier of Peru.

"I shall at once attack Tumbez," said he. The forces accordingly embarked, and directed their course to that city on the coast.

Sailing in between Puna (a city off the coast) and Tumbez, Pizarro's vessels were met by canoes filled with natives. "Welcome, welcome" said they, as the vessels drew near. "We come to invite you to land upon our island and remain with us as our guests."

You may be sure Pizarro did not wait to be urged. Nothing was more to his mind than that a city of Peru should be entered under such delightful circumstances. What the circumstances might be under which, by and by, either he or the natives would be forced to leave, he did not so much care at present.

On reaching the island, the Spaniards were met by crowds and crowds of natives dressed in rich aud gaudy cloaks, covered with gold and precious stones. Such deafening music, too, as burst forth when Pizarro landed. Such prancing about and capering! Such howling and singing! — all in honor of the strange white people who had come, borne over the waters by the great white birds.

This hearty reception delighted Pizarro's ambitious soul; for, knowing that these Puna Indians were bitter enemies of Tumbez, he thought he saw here a chance to work this enmity to his own advantage.

But these natives were wiser than he thought. They, too, could play a part, as Pizarro soon learned.

For several days Pizarro's men rested and feasted on this pleasant island, lording it over the simple-hearted natives in a way that no doubt was vastly agreeable to the Spaniards. But one day a servant of Pizarro's came to him and said, " I have a suspicion that these natives are not what they seem. I have a suspicion that under all their seeming friendship there is plotting of some sort against us."

Pizarro was startled. At once he called his officers together and set out into the village. Sure enough! there in the village were the natives hard at work making hosts of arrows and javelins. In the forests was the cacique himself, drilling his people and preparing them for an attack upon their unwelcome guests. Surely, the Puna men were not as foolish and simple-hearted as they had seemed.

No time was to be lost. Quickly summoning his men, an attack was made upon the house of the cacique. He himself was captured, and his house ransacked and robbed of its jewels and fine cloths.

The natives fled in dismay. But Pizarro knew that no time was to be lost. The natives would revenge themselves for the capture of their chief. All night the Spaniards watched, ready to engage in battle. At daybreak a great noise arose from the forests, and down upon the Spanish camp burst the Indians, clanging their war instruments, and shouting and yelling, until the very arch of heaven seemed to ring.

Instantly the Spaniards sent forth a volley of fire upon them. It was a short, fierce encounter; but the natives, with all their numbers, were no match for the cool-headed, skilful Spaniards with their deadly fire.

The Indians turned and fled. Pizarro's men followed, pouring out their fire and striking down their foes at every step. Then followed a sickening day of wretched plunder, destruction and deadly havoc. Those natives who escaped capture or massacre fled to the mainland. Nothing remained now but to deal with the cacique and the other prisoners. In the trial that followed Pizarro sternly commanded that the prisoners be put to death, all except the cacique; he should be spared on this one condition — that he pledge himself ever after to act as an ally of the Spaniards, using always his influence in their behalf.

The first step towards the "Conquest of Peru" had now been taken. Next in order should be the attack on Tumbez. So, getting together his plunder, he sent that ahead on rafts, and prepared to follow with his army and his supplies. In a few hours Pizarro was again in the harbor of Tumbez, on the very margin of the empire — the land of the Incas.

Pizarro Invades Peru.

If Pizarro had fancied that his old friends at Tumbez were still his friends, and that they were mildly awaiting his arrival, he was doomed to sad disappointment and to no little unpleasant surprise ; for, on drawing near the shore, and seeing nothing of his rafts, he learned all too quickly that they had been captured by the natives, assisted no doubt by those Puna Indians who had escaped from the island.

Pizarro hastened into the city. Here, instead of the throng of curious natives who had met him in so friendly a manner on his visit a few months before, he found only deserted streets and buildings. Scouts were at once sent out, and soon it was learned that, with the treasures of their own city, as well as those taken from the rafts, the people had fled into the forests.

Setting out after them, their camp was soon found, their cacique taken prisoner and the natives put to flight.

"Shame upon you, traitor, to treat my men like this ! You, who on my last visit here pretended such friendship for the Spaniard ! What, pray, did I do on my first visit here that you should turn against me like this ? "

The cacique trembled with fear. His eyes grew big, his teeth chattered, his knees knocked together, his very hair seemed to stand erect.

"I beg you, great stranger," said he, keeping his eyes fixed in terror on the great guns, "spare me. It was not I. It was my chiefs who did this."

" Where, then, are the chiefs?" asked Pizarro scornfully.

"I — I know not. They — they are fled."

"Put him in irons," ordered Pizarro. "We will not kill him. He may be of more use to us alive than dead."

On the following day Pizarro assembled his men, and said to them, "We are now in the lands of the Incas. There are great dangers and great difficulties before us. There are mountains to cross. There are thirst and hunger to be endured — perhaps sickness and death. There are not very many of us, and we do not know how great our foe may be; but we have firearms and skill and courage. Have we the spirit to go on, to fight, to suffer, to die perhaps — all for the glorious hope of enrolling our names in history as the conquerors of Peru?"

"Long live our captain! Long live Pizarro! Long

live the future governor of Peru! Lead on. We will follow. Lead on! lead on!" cried his brave followers.

Then the march began. "Straight at the heart of the Incas let us strike, and that, too, at once," said Pizarro.

In from the coast, up the mountains, across deserts and through rich valleys the brave little band marched, until at last the garrisoned towns of the Incas were reached. On every side the Spaniards were met with kindness from the natives, and often with personal welcome from the cacique.

At last the city of Zaran was reached. Here Pizarro learned that a little further on the Indians were drawn up in battle array. What did this mean? Had the Inca's suspicions been aroused? Was a combat with these natives now so close at hand?

Pizarro was prudent as well as daring. He had no men to lose in needless risk, neither did he wish to shrink from battle, if that was the Inca's meaning. Accordingly he sent De Soto, his lieutenant, forward with a body of chosen men to reconnoitre. Two weeks passed, and no word came. Pizarro, fearing they had been massacred, was just on the eve of starting forth in search of them when, to his great joy, De Soto appeared. With him was a tall, noble-looking Indian, brilliantly dressed in a richly-bejewelled robe and many chains of gold.

PERUVIAN STONE IDOL AND WATER-POTS FOUND 62 FEET UNDER GROUND.

"This," said De Soto, "is the brother of the Inca. He comes as messenger from the Inca himself. He brings with him as presents from the royal chief these beautiful, finely-woven, many-colored cloths, these sheep, these birds, besides this honey, this gold, and these silver vases and precious stones."

Pizarro welcomed his royal guest with the respect becoming one of so great a name, talked with him and made him presents of a red cap and some long strings of bright-colored beads.

" I come," said he, " from the Inca to bid you welcome to our land, and invite you to visit him at his camp."

Pizarro, with great show of delight and appreciation of the mighty Inca's condescension, accepted this invitation, and took great pains to make the guest's visit a pleasant one, and to make such a display of his army and of his power that the Inca should be impressed with the report the messenger would make on his return. Pizarro was not, however, at all deceived by this appearance of friendship, and saw at once that the messenger had been sent merely as a spy.

Pizarro Advances Upon the Incas.

Pizarro had pushed on to the foot of the mighty Cordilleras, on the other side of which he knew lay the fertile plains and beautiful cities of the Inca. On the water-side these mountains, indeed, looked grim and forbidding. On the other side were gentle slopes and beautiful woody spots. Here and there, up among the hills on the tops of rounded mounds, were perched the odd little villages of the Peruvians, each with its shining temple and its great strong walls.

It was at the city of Caxamalca that the Inca held his court ; and it was on a gently-sloping plain outside the city that his army was drawn up.

The messenger had returned from Pizarro's camp, and though he had reported the terrible power of the Spanish firearms, and had described the great animals, larger by far than sheep and much more swift, on which the Spaniards rode, the Inca was little moved by fear as he looked proudly over his numberless followers, brave and daring, strong and well trained, and, above all, so loyal to their country and to him.

"Let them come," said he. "Little can they do with their two hundred men against my unnumbered forces."

We will meet them, and if they are hostile they will die. Are we not children of the Sun, and is that not enough ?

Let it not be said that children of the Sun have fear."

The Inca had make up his mind to get Pizarro into his power by trickery. That was the Peruvian method of procedure in battle, and in this method the Inca had perfect faith. He did not know that in the Spaniard he had a foe whose duplicity could more than match his own.

Long, long ago, a dying Inca had told his people that one day there would come from the far east a band of strangers, " white, with long, straight beards," who would conquer and put an end to the great empire of the Incas. But this prophecy was not remembered now, and the Inca retired to his rest in perfect contentment, assured within himself that there was little cause for fear from these foreign foes.

The march across the mountains had been full of hardships. In some places the mountain road was a mere path, so narrow that the soldiers must go forward one by one, carefully leading their horses. Deep ravines and steep precipices added to the difficulty. Colder and colder grew the air as they went higher and higher up the mountain side. The summit was at last reached, fires were built, and the weary little band rested and warmed themselves.

Here, upon this mountain top, came again an envoy from the Inca, repeating the same invitation and welcome.

Pizarro was puzzled. Not once, in his march up the mountain, had he received anything but kindness from the villages through which he had passed. What did it mean? Was the Inca so foolish as to suppose the Spaniards came with any other than the object of conquest? Had he thus easily given up in terror to them, and was this his chosen way to receive his conquerors? Or was he wise and wily, and was all this pretence at friendliness but a deep plot to decoy the Spaniards beyond the mountains into the city, and there destroy them?

In this second visit the envoy unwisely told Pizarro of a feud existing between Atahualpa, the Inca at Caxamalca, and his brother Hauscar, the Inca of another part of the country. Pizarro was shrewd; and at once saw in this a possibility for securing aid in this attack upon Peru.

THE CITY OF THE INCAS.

The march down the mountain side was slow and full of difficulties. To climb the steep precipices with their horses and their heavy armor had been hard enough ; but to descend these slippery steeps, with the yawning chasms beneath, was more frightful still. But this little band of tried soldiers knew not the meaning of fear. On they pressed, down into the beautiful green valley in which lay the shining city of the Inca.

Here, indeed, lay stretched out before them the rich lands of that empire whose conquest had so long been the one bright dream of Pizarro's life. There lay the city. Beyond moved the marshalled forces of the great Inca himself. Pizarro realized that his glory or his destruction, his victory or his defeat was close at hand.

As yet no sign of resistance was evident. Again a messenger from the Inca welcomed them, and brought them food and rich gifts. Pizarro's heart sank within him as he noted the enormous forces of the Inca drawn up beyond the city and compared with them his own little band of two hundred. But it was only for a moment. With grim determination he gave his order, "March!"

Up to the very gates of the city they moved — in through the gates — up to the public square. And still no resistance. The city was deserted, the houses closed. Pizarro was indeed in possession of the city of the Inca.

" We must lose no time," said Pizarro to De Soto, "in finding out the real intentions of this mysterious Inca. In the morning, with fifteen horsemen, you shall proceed to the Inca's camp and demand a hearing."

Early with the rising of the sun De Soto set forth.

Atahualpa had been told of their approach. He allowed him to come into his presence and to deliver the message from Pizarro. During it all, the Inca sat motionless, not a muscle of his face showing in any way that he was conscious of a stranger's presence.

" Is he deaf and dumb," said one of the horsemen, "or is he made of stone?"

A long, deep silence followed De Soto's speech. De Soto waited. The whole court waited. The Inca sat motionless.

" This must be the Peruvian idea of noble dignity," said one horseman to another.

By and by, a tall, swarthy-faced nobleman advanced and said, " It is well."

Then followed another long silence. At last, Hernando, one of Pizarro's brothers who had come with him, spoke sharply and said, " We do not come here to trifle. We demand an answer. What is the reception intended by the Inca for the Spaniards?"

DE SOTO IN THE INCAS CAMP.

At this, the Inca slowly raised his head in a grieved, injured sort of way and said, "This is our feast day. To-morrow I will visit your leader."

REGAL EMBLEMS AND HOUSEHOLD GODS.

The Inca again dropped his head, as much as to say, "Trouble me no more." Quietly the horsemen left the camp and returned to Pizarro. The report of the wealth, the strength, the discipline, and the great numbers of natives drawn up in readiness for battle, aroused fear in the hearts of many a brave Spaniard, as he contrasted the two armies.

Pizarro himself knew that fearful odds were against him. "And still," said he to his men, "the arts of war do not consist wholly in battles. We have our firearms and we have our wits. Let us put them both to work. Can we not fall upon our foe, and, by some great stratagem like that with which Cortes overthrew the mighty Montezuma, bring them into our power. Escape, there is none. Of that we are sure. Then let us *act.*"

That night, as Pizarro lay beneath the starry Southern sky, he rehearsed to himself over and over the desperate bravery of his kinsman, Cortes. "His position was not unlike mine, and he seized upon the king," said he to himself. Then calling his officers together, he said: "Comrades, I have a desperate plan, one that becomes our desperate position. To battle with our small force against the Inca would be folly. To attempt retreat would be death. Even if we did reach Panama again there would be for us only sneers and jeers. Our only hope lies in a bold stroke — in strategy. Here is my plan. To morrow the Inca comes to our camp. I shall take him prisoner."

"Take the Inca prisoner!" cried his officers starting up. "It can't be done."

"It *can* be done." answered Pizarro, calmly. Can we not do as much as Cortes did in Mexico? Did he not with a little force take Montezuma prisoner? Can we not do the same?"

"It is desperate, it is perilous, it is hopeless," said his officers.

"Is not our position here desperate, perilous, and hopeless?" answered he.

Capture of Atahualpa.

All was in readiness in the Spanish camp. Pizarro's desperate scheme had been communicated to the soldiers, the plan for action arranged, and a signal agreed upon.

It was nearly night-fall before the Inca came. All day

long his forces were mysteriously parading up and down the road leading from their camp to the city, much to the annoyance and concern of Pizarro, who feared his scheme might fail from lack of opportunity. Message after message came from the Inca, who, as if filled with presentiment of the fate in store for him, seemed determined to take every precaution in entering the city.

But at last, borne upon a gorgeous litter, and surrounded by a strong guard, he entered the city. As he paused in the great square, a priest advanced to him, Bible in hand, and said, "I am a priest and I am a teacher of Christians. In this Book are the Commandments of God. I ask you in His name to be friendly with us."

Atahualpa, seeing the book, took it from the priest's hand, looked at for an instant, then threw it upon the ground. He was no longer the dignified, solemn Inca. His rage burst forth. Dignity was forgotten. "I know," shouted he, "only too well how you have treated my people and have robbed my villages. Now I come to meet the Spaniard, face to face, and to tell him that I will have my treasures restored to me. I do not leave this place until all are brought and laid at my feet."

The monk tried to speak. " Silence ! " thundered the Inca. " and hear *me*. I will not be slave to any king. I will be friends with you, but I will never obey your king. Neither will I bow to your God. I am a child of the Sun. I will not know your God. The Sun, the Sun is our God, and him will his children worship."

The monk, angry at this, turned to Pizarro, saying, " Seize the infidel ! Seize him ! He insults our Bible and our God ! Seize him ! Seize him !.

Instantly Pizarro gave the signal and rushed upon the Inca. A great cry went up from the square. Guns blazed forth their deadly fire ! The cannon roared ! Soldiers burst forth from every side and fell upon the unprotected guard. Out came the cavalry, charging fiercely upon the frightened natives. A panic ensued. Order was lost. Confusion reigned. The tramping, foaming horses seemed to the poor natives, fiends indeed. The square ran blood. The shrieks of the wounded and dying, mingled with the thunder of the cannon, filled the air. The cavaliers, slashing right and left with their sabres, mowed down the Peruvians like grain before the mower's scythe. Around the sacred body of the Inca thronged his guard, fighting fiercely to

have his precious life. One by one they fell before the fury
of the Spaniards. One rush upon the bearers of the litter
and it fell upon the writhing bodies of its dying defenders.

Now the blood-thirsty Spaniards fell upon the Inca.
"Away, away!" cried Pizarro. "Preserve the Inca's life!
Do you not see we must hold him as hostage? Away,
away with him! To kill him would be our ruin."

Poor, crest-fallen Atahualpa! As they led him away he
walked as one in a dream — dazed, unconscious. His beautiful feathers were broken, his crown lost, his robe dab-
bled and blood-stained. All his glory was gone. Atahualpa, the Inca, the child of the Sun, was a prisoner of war.

The Inca was conducted to Pizarro's own apartments, and
there dressed in simple garments. As with sad and
wretched face he took the seat beside his captor, Pizarro
said to him, "Listen, O thou great Inca, and know that we
are subjects of a greater king than you. We come to conquer your country and bend you to our king. We come
to make Christians of you and teach you the wickedness of
your heathen worship."

The Inca made no reply; he only slowly shook his head,
puzzled, sorrowful, crushed.

"You have nothing to fear, Atahualpa," continued Piz
arro, "if only you will submit yourselves to us. We mak
war only on our foes. You will be protected and kindl;
dealt with if you are true to us." Then, calling his mei
together, he commended them for their valor, and cautione(
them to be watchful lest the Peruvians fall upon then
unawares, in their desperation and determination to rescu(
their sacred Inca.

Then the soldiers retired to their posts, and quiet reigned
The day's work was done. The Inca was captured. Bu
what will the morrow bring?

ATAHUALPA A PRISONER.

The morning sun rose warm and clear, seemingly al
unconscious of the terrible slaughter of its children, anc
careless of the sacrilegious capture of its chosen ruler.

It was with a strange sense of loss of confidence in th(
Sun-god that Atahualpa and his fellow captives per
formed their morning devotions, and prayed for protectioi
through the coming day.

With the first rays of light, the captives were marshalled forth into the public square. Oh, such a ghastly sight! There on every side, their rich robes stained with blood, lay two thousand of Inca's bravest nobles, stiff and stark in death.

"These warriors are to be buried, even while their Sun-god's face looks down upon them," said Pizarro. "See to it that trenches are dug, and that these captives bury their own dead. Let them see how little power their Sun-god has before the soldiers of the Spanish king."

It seems cruel and coarse in Pizarro to have made this thrust at the already broken-spirited captives; but great heroes of Pizarro's type are not apt to be burdened with an over-sensitive nature, and then, too, it was the custom of the time to have little mercy upon the conquered foe.

Pizarro knew that his victory must at once be followed up with another onslaught before the people were recovered from their confusion and terror.

To have taken their Inca, the child of the Sun, was a deed unheard of in all their history. That the Inca was under the divine protection of the Sun and could *never* see misfortune, was their religion. Now all was swept away.

The loss of two thousand warriors was nothing. They held it their duty and their privilege to fight and die for their country and their Inca. But to see their Inca taken prisoner, captured — perhaps killed — that was a death-blow to their very faith, and it filled them with superstitious fear.

While this terror was upon them, Pizarro knew was his time to strike. Accordingly he despatched his horsemen to the Peruvian camp. The camp was indeed in sad confusion. The thousands of troops, one half of whom alone could have destroyed, ten times over, the little Spanish army had they made an attack upon it, were rushing hither and thither, groaning and wailing, prostrating themselves before the uprising sun, begging and praying for mercy. Their god had deserted them! Their monarch was slain! What was there for them but flight?

Up rode the little body of horsemen into the very heart of the camp. Away fled the natives as before avenging fiends, leaving their camp and all its treasures in the possession of the Spaniards.

In the Inca's gorgeous tent such treasures of gold and brilliant stones were found! All these the cavaliers gathered together and laid at Pizarro's feet. Even the greedy Spaniards for once were satisfied with their gain. Had they returned to Panama with this treasure alone, they would even then have brought to the Spanish power a world of wealth, and have secured for themselves lives of ease and luxury. But "Conquest! conquest!" was their watchword.

Pizarro amused himself during the weeks that followed, in conversing with his royal prisoner, and in teaching him to speak the Spanish language. In nothing did the Inca show such interest as in this. To him it was his one hope of learning the Spanish secrets, and so sometime, perhaps, freeing himself from their hated power.

The manner in which the Spaniards were able to read was great puzzle to Atahualpa. Nothing pleased and amused him more than to have a word written for him, and then to take it from one Spaniard to another asking, "What do these figures say?" And when one after another of the Spaniards would read the word, giving the same name to it, the Inca would go away both delighted and puzzled at this strange power. One day, it is said, he presented a word to Pizarro himself, saying, "Read, read!" Pizarro looked at it, grew red in the face, and was obliged to admit that he could not read. The Inca looked at him with scorn, and never after did he have such profound reverence for his captor.

PIZARRO'S TREACHERY.

Some few weeks after his capture the Inca said to Pizarro, "I have a brother in a neighboring province. If you will free me, I will give him into your power — he and all his belongings — and will bring to you loads of golden plate and bars of silver, more than would fill this palace."

Pizarro's interest was aroused — his greed was aroused too, I fancy. After some show of authority and pretence at refusal, Pizarro agreed to the Inca's offer. Away went the Inca's trusty servant to the city of Cuzco with the Inca's message that two thousand men should at once come to Pizarro, bringing all the treasure they could carry.

In a short time the treasure began to arrive. Such loads of gold! Such jewels! Again even the Spanish

reed was more than satisfied. " What manner of country can this be," said they, "to pour out such wealth from
is cities? Let us hasten on to complete our conquest of
his wonderful country."

Hernando, Pizarro's brother, set forth across the country
) this city of Cuzco. Accompanied by guides under
rders from the Inca, Hernando and his men were
verywhere met with generous welcome, and were sump-
tuously feasted. In one city they shattered the great
idol, stripped a temple of its glory, and bade the people
save their heathen worship and worship the true God. A
strange way of turning peoples' hearts God-ward, we should
say; but many things were strange in those early times.

The horrified Peruvians looked on as the Spaniards razed
their idols and their temples, expecting every instant that a
bolt from the sky would strike them dead. But no bolt
came. The sun seemed not to care. What did it all mean?
Had they not always preserved and protected these idols
reverently and carefully; and had they not been taught
that the sun-god would most terribly avenge any injury or
insult to them? Who were the Spaniards that even the
sun dared not punish them?

Just about this time Almagro arrived from Panama. Pizarro had promised him that as soon as he should have established himself in Peru he would send for his old friend, and would divide the power with him. Almagro, having more confidence in Pizarro's courage than in his honesty, thought it quite time that he came to Peru to remind Pizarro of his promise. Pizarro pretended great joy at the sight of his old friend, and eagerly unfolded to him the story of his success, and his plans for the future.

But the ransom which the Inca had promised had now all been brought, and the Inca demanded his freedom. Now, Pizarro had no more idea of freeing the Inca than he had of going back to Panama and settling down upon his farm. He knew full well that the Inca would raise an army and march against the Spaniards at once, and that all Peru would flock around his banner. But he had not hesitated to lie to the Inca, and to receive his great ransom under these false pretences. Pizarro was not the man to hesitate in a little question of right or wrong. He was there to conquer Peru, and to him no means were beneath his use.

Pizarro was distant and cold to the Inca now, and often surly and cruel. He knew he had acted contemptibly

ith his prisoner, and so shrank from meeting him, much
more from speaking with him.

"I must find some pretence for this breaking of my
promise," said Pizarro; "even with a heathen captive it is
well to have some excuse."

Rumor now reached the city that a mighty army was
advancing to attack the Spaniards, and that the army had
been raised by private messages from the Inca. In this
army, so rumor said, were thirty thousand Peruvians and
two thousand Carib man-eaters. A terrible force, indeed,
if the report was true. At any rate, Pizarro saw in it an
opportunity to seize upon Atahualpa. He ordered him to
be brought forth. "What is the meaning of this treason?"
said he. "Have I not treated you with honor? Have you
not been protected and generously treated? Had I not
promised you freedom? Why have you thus turned against
me?"

"I do not even know what you mean," answered the Inca,
wearily. "Am I not in your power? You yourself shall
say whether I have been protected, whether I have been
justly dealt with."

It is said Pizarro quailed before the quiet contempt of his

royal prisoner. But if he did, it was but for a moment. Turning to a servant, he said, "Take away this prisoner and keep him closely guarded. He shall be dealt with by and by."

Enough had been said to arouse the fiery Spaniards against the Inca. Now there arose a clamor in the camp that Pizarro could not have quieted had he wished. "The Inca has caused this peril," said the soldiers, "and he shall be brought forth. He should be tried. He should be slain."

DEATH OF ATAHUALPA.

Pizarro led forth the unhappy Atahualpa for trial. The trial was but a mere form, for already his doom was sealed. He was placed upon a bench before his cruel judges, Pizarro and Almagro. Little was said, for there was little to be said. The Inca was to die — that was the only thought — not because treason could be proven against him, but because it was convenient for his captors that he be put out of the way.

Such a brief, one-sided trial was a mere farce ; and Ata-
ualpa was condemned to be burned at the stake.

Poor Atahualpa ! little had he deserved this cruel fate ! a
good, kind ruler, over a loyal and loving people, he had
risen in rebellion only at the invasion of his country by
his people's foe.

"What have I done," said he, the tears rolling down his
warthy cheeks, "that you should put me to such a death
as this? Have you not been welcomed everywhere by
my subjects, befriended by them, enriched by them? Have
I not lavished my wealth upon you? Have mercy! I, the
once powerful Inca of Peru, I, the child of the Sun, beg
you to have mercy!"

Pizarro, be it said to his credit, strode out of the hall, his
hard heart touched by the truth of the Inca's words. But
his resolve was not changed. Hardly had the sun reached
the western sky when the Inca was brought forth, chained
hand and foot, into the city square. His face was proud
and kingly ; his carriage stately. Not one word, one look
of pleading now. Before these treacherous Spaniards he
walked, a king again. The fagots were piled about him.
the priest advanced to perform the rites of baptism ; to

offer him the choice of burning or of strangling; and thus
closed the life of Atahualpa, the child of the Sun.

Prescott, in his history of Peru, gives this account of the
funeral of the Inca :

" The body of the Inca remained on the place of execu-
tion through the night.   On the following morning it was
removed to the church of San Francisco, where his funeral
obsequies were performed with great solemnity.   Pizarro
and the principal cavaliers went into mourning, and the
troops listened with devout attention, to the service of the
dead from the lips of Father Valverde.   The ceremony was
interrupted by the sound of loud cries, and wailing of
many voices at the doors of the church.   These were suddenly thrown open, and a number of Indian women, the
wives and sisters of the deceased, rushing up the great
aisle, surrounded the corpse.   This was not the way, they
cried, to celebrate the rites of an Inca, and they declared
their intention to sacrifice themselves on his tomb, and bear
him company to the land of spirits.   The audience, out-
raged by this frantic behavior, told the intruders that
Atahualpa had died in the faith of a Christian, and that the
God of the Christians abhorred such sacrifices.   They then

aused the women to be excluded from the church, and
veral, retiring to their own quarters, killed themselves in
ie vain hope of accompanying their beloved lord to the
right mansions of the Sun.

Pizarro's Capture of Cuzco.

When rumor came of the great force marching upon the
Spaniards, De Soto had been sent out to reconnoitre.
Now, when Atahualpa had but just been buried, De Soto
and his scouts rode back into the city, bearing the news
that no such army was to be found, and that the whole
report was but a false one. Everywhere he had found the
people kindly disposed, willing to share with the Spaniards
and to aid them.

At this report, Pizarro was, for a time, filled with shame
and remorse. "But it cannot be helped," said he grimly,
"and after all, it would never have been quite safe with
him alive. If he did not in this case instigate insurrection,
he might have done it later." And so Pizarro easily satis-

fied his not over-sensitive conscience, and went on with his plans for attacking Cuzco.

Leaving a few soldiers in charge, he set forth across the slopes of the mountains to the Peruvian capital.

It was not a hard journey; and although twice they were attacked by hostile Peruvians, the small band reached the capital with little difficulty.

During the journey, Pizarro's suspicions were aroused against an old chief who had been captured by his forces, and he was at once condemned to be burned alive. As he stood in the midst of the fagots, the priest besought him to accept the Spanish religion and so save his own soul. But the poor chief, who perhaps in his whole life had never seen such selfishness, such greed, such lawless plunder and slaughter as he had seen in the Spanish quarters, turned wearily away saying, "Alas, I see nothing in your religion that seems better than my own worship of the Sun. We have been a gentle, prosperous, peace-loving people, and our sun-god has given us warmth and protection." Then turning his face toward the bright sun that shone down upon him, he endured the torture without one sign of suffering, and so passed out from the persecution of the Spanish conquerors.

PIZARRO'S ENTRY INTO CUZCO.

As Pizarro marched on towards the capital, he was met by a Peruvian noble, who said, "I am Manco the brother of the murdered Inca. and I am the rightful successor to the power. I come to you as a friend, and I ask your aid and protection in my attempt to come into the authority that belongs to me."

The shrewd Pizarro saw at once in this a help for himself. "You are welcome," said he, "and I promise you my aid in your attempt to secure your royal rights. Let us go forward together."

It was night when the Spaniards reached the city. There being no signs of hostility, Pizarro rested until morning outside the gates. When the bright sun rose, Pizarro divided his forces into three lines, and with waving plumes and banners, glittering armor, and sounding trumpets, marched in through the great gateway.

The people seemed dazed by such display of glory. Then, as the young prince came, borne upon the royal litter, the people shouted and waved their turbans, hailing him as their sovereign.

You may be sure Pizarro lost no time in taking possession of the city and establishing his power. He at once marched to the central square and took possession of the

PIZARRO'S HOUSE AT CUZCO.

93

great buildings on every side for his officers. From the towers and the domes floated the Spanish flag. No hostility appeared on the part of the people, and Pizarro seemed indeed to have completed the "conquest of Peru." The soldiers, eager for more treasures, ransacked the public buildings, tore the golden frescoes from the walls of the temples, and even entered the sacred vaults of the dead, robbing them of the funeral ornaments and golden urns.

At once Pizarro had young Manco crowned as Inca, and in the presence of the throng, he and the young prince pledged friendship and everlasting loyalty.

He set up a new government, in which he held the real power, and retained as much show of the old forms as seemed necessary to avoid arousing suspicion among the natives.

But though the conquest had been so easily accomplished and Cuzco was already a Spanish city, there was little peace for Pizarro. Hardly had he taken possession when reports of gathering armies reached his ears. Almagro, however, went against them, and so perfect was the rout on one occasion that the natives turned and killed their own chief, so angry were they at his failure.

But these attacks from the natives, which were frequent, were as nothing compared with a contest which seemed about to come, and that too with his own countrymen.

All this time, Alvarado, the governor of Panama, had been seeking information regarding Pizarro's proceedings in Peru. And when he heard of his marvellous success and of the fabulous wealth of the conquered country, his ambition and greed were fired.

Getting together five hundred troops, he sailed for the southern sea, intending to take possession of the northern part of Peru, and, if need be, dispute his right with Pizarro.

Grievous misfortune assailed him, however; and by the time he had crossed the mountains, in the freezing cold, he had lost fully one-half his men and horses in the awful chasms, the provisions were giving out, sickness seized upon them, and little courage remained to attack Cuzco.

In the valley they were met by Almagro, who had been sent by Pizarro to treat with, and if need be, fight the new-comers. At first there was great show of resistance on the part of Alvarado, but it was of little avail. Almagro came into his camp, offering to escort him as a friend to Cuzco, and to share with him the treasures gathered in the city.

While Almagro and Alvarado conversed together, the soldiers, too, were mingling freely and talking of their adventures. It was a strange conciliation; in a few hours both armies were marching along together to the capital, and once more Pizarro was rescued from an impending evil.

Almagro Against Pizarro.

Pizarro now planned to found a new city. "No one," said he, "but Indians would think of locating their capital all this distance from the sea. It may have served very well over here behind the mountains for the natives; but we must have a sea-port. There will be commerce for the future of Peru!"

Accordingly, in the beautiful valley of the Rimac River, Pizarro began his work of founding the city which we now call Lima, but which he called "The City of the King."

It was a beautiful city as he planned it. The streets were wide and straight, and the great square in the centre was surrounded by elegant buildings, one of which Pizarro appropriated for his own mansion.

Such swarms of workmen as he employed! The city

ew up out of the plain, like magic. Around it was built
strong clay wall, high enough to keep out the foe, and
rong enough to resist the shocks of those terrible earth-
uakes which so often in that latitude shake the cities to
neir very foundations.

This new city was Pizarro's one delight. Giving Cuzco
nto the command of Almagro, he himself remained in the
ew capital, watching with eager interest every new build-
ng, and superintending, with wise thought for the city's
nture, the laying out of each street and square.

All this time Pizarro had noticed that Almagro was not
content. There was a sullen look in his face, and now and
nen there flashed in his eyes a light that warned Pizarro
f a time when Almagro would demand of him the division of spoils and of power which had been promised
nim.

Pizarro was quick to see, and very likely, too, his sense of
nis own unfairness helped to sharpen his wits. At any
nate, Pizarro thought it wise to make some concession to
Almagro — some show of intention to abide by his promise.
t would have been well had he thought of this a little
narlier, for now, even while he was debating, Hernando,

who had been sent to Spain to tell of the wonderful country now held by Pizarro. returned to Peru.

He had been received with great honor, and had brought back most generous rewards from the delighted king. Upon Pizarro he conferred the governorship of Peru, with power to make conquests two hundred miles further south; to Hernando himself, he had granted permission to raise forces to return to Peru with him, and had made him a knight of the royal court ; and to Almagro he gave permission to conquer and hold for his own six hundred miles of territory south of Pizarro's dominion.

Now. when Almagro heard this, he at once claimed that Cuzco itself was within the limits of the territory granted to him by the king.   A bitter quarrel arose between Almagro and Juan and Gonzalo. Pizarro's two brothers, who had been in command of Cuzco before Almagro came.

Pizarro was sent for by speedy messengers.   He sent back word to his brothers to hold the city, and he himself would return at once.   When at last he reached the city, he greeted Almagro with all the warmth of an old friend, put on an air of reproachful sadness that Almagro should have doubted his honest intention to make a just division with

im when the new capital had been finished, and succeeded
nce more in bringing Almagro to friendly terms.

MANCO, THE YOUNG INCA.

You have not forgotten the young Inca, who, all this time
had been pretending to rule his people, though he himself
was ruled by Pizarro. So meek and pliable had he been
that Pizarro had almost ceased to think of any possible re-
pellion from him.

But Pizarro little knew what was going on under Manco's
appearance of submission.

He was like his predecessors, proud and courageous, and
full of reverence for the religion of his people. Imagine
then the rebellious spirit with which he saw his mild and
thrifty people under the oppression of a foreign foe, and the
horror with which he saw his temples destroyed and the
idols torn from their sacred places.

During all these months, while seeming to willingly co-
operate with Pizarro in all his plans for the future glory of

Peru, he had nourished a secret plan of escape. Once out among his people, he knew he could arouse them to a sense of their position, raise numberless troops, rush upon the city and rescue it from the foreign foe.

For some time he had been sending secret messages to all parts of his kingdom, bidding them to prepare for war against the tyrant Pizarro.

Now all was ready. From every village answer had come telling him of his people's readiness to follow him in any plan that should free them from their oppression, and restore their temples and their gods to their rightful glory.

And so, one night Manco dressed himself as a peasant, slipped out of the palace, and hastened to a thicket of low brush outside the city. Success seemed to attend him. But alas, hardly had he reached his hiding-place before the galloping of horses told him he was pursued. A moment more, and the barking of the dogs told Juan Pizarro, who led the party, that the young prince was discovered.

Poor Manco, discouraged for the time, and bitterly disappointed that the armies awaiting him must lay down their arms and wait again, went sadly back to the city, from which so few hours ago he had hastened with such eager hope.

He was taken at once to a strong tower and surrounded by
a guard. For a time it looked as if the young prince's
cause was lost.

But when Hernando returned from Spain he said, "Re-
lease the young prince. It is cruel and altogether un-
necessary. Most bitterly do I repent the death of Atahu-
lpa. Let us not repeat that cruelty."

And thus it came about that Manco was again restored
to his freedom in the palace; but all those weeks of
imprisonment had not served to increase the prince's love
or the Spaniards, nor had it weakened in him his firm determination to rescue his people. He only awaited another
opportunity to attempt their deliverance.

MANCO'S ESCAPE.

One day Manco said to Hernando, "You are in need of
more gold. Pizarro needs it in his new cities. You need
t for your army. Far up in the mountains there is a secret
cave known only to the Incas. Send me secretly to this

cave, and I will bring you jewels grander than you have
ever seen, gold purer than you have ever melted."

Hernando had great faith in the fidelity of this young
prince; and now, too, his never-satisfied greed for gold
was excited. "Larger jewels, purer gold," thought he.
"I must risk it. If the prince is playing me double, I can
easily seize him and bring him again into my power. I will
send him."

Away Manco went, accompanied by two Spaniards who,
since they were subject to his leading, were as good as no
guard at all. As we might easily guess, he led them straight
to a loyal Peruvian town, delivered them up, and at once
himself took command of the little army awaiting him.
Then fleet messengers were sent into every village and
town to announce the young prince's escape, and to bid
them gather their forces.

Ten days passed by. Eagerly, impatiently and somewhat fearfully Hernando awaited the young prince's return.
A Spaniard who had been out about the country saw sus-
picious signs of uprising among the people. He hastened
to Hernando with the news.

"It is Manco!" exclaimed he. "I was a fool to trust

m. But he must be overtaken. Juan, Juan, gather
:ty horsemen and set forth with all haste to overtake this
yal fugitive. Let there be no delay. Haste, haste I
fy !"

And away galloped Juan out upon the highway, straight
t the mountains.

Hardly had he gone five miles before he was met by the
vo Spaniards who had accompanied Manco, galloping at
,.ll speed towards Cuzco. "Come back to the city ! Come
ack to the city !" cried they, breathless and frightened.
The Peruvians have arisen ! They are in pursuit ! There
re millions of them ! And Manco is at their head !"

"Go to the city and tell Hernando," answered Juan.
Go with all haste. And tell him, too, that I will go on
nd perhaps be able to hold them back. Come on, my
nen, come on !" And away the sixty horsemen flew to meet
he troops of angry Peruvians.

"There they are, there they are !" cried Juan, "on the
opposite side of the river ! Ready, ready, my comrades, plunge in, and follow me ! Our only hope is in
rushing upon them with such fury that, as at Caxamalca,
they will be struck with panic."

Into the rushing river, with all the rash courage of a hot-headed Spaniard, Juan plunged. One second, and the river seemed alive with Spanish horses and riders. The Peruvians looked on aghast. A hot, hard fight and they are driven back into the forest. Once more the white man is victorious.

"We will encamp here upon the plain," said Juan. "This is not the end of these Peruvians, I fear."

And, indeed, it was not. With the first rays of light a sight met Juan's eyes which might well strike terror to his heart. The mountains seemed alive. As far as eye could reach, on every table-land and through every defile, shone the javelins of Peruvian warriors. Without warning, down upon the little Spanish company they showered arrows and stones.

Another hard battle. Hour after hour the brave horsemen stood amid the Peruvian host, now advancing, now retreating. But the natives poured in from the towns on all sides, faster and faster, thicker and thicker. There was no hope of driving back such a numberless throng. "Retreat!" called Juan; and rushing down to the river banks, they hurried across and back to the city.

Here, at the city gates, more terror greeted him. All round the city as far as eye could reach, so it seemed to man, were troops and troops of Peruvians, seething like a great sea, all pushing on towards the city gates. The people were aroused at last. Cuzco was beseiged!

"There is but one way to enter, comrades," said Juan, grimly; "and that is to dash through the swarm, trample these warriors beneath our horses' feet and rush in through the gates while the panic is upon them." Poor, slow-thinking Peruvians! It was upon their sad lack of cool-headedness, as we call it, together with their superstition, that the Spaniards based their operations.

The Seige of Cuzco.

Morning came. From the city watch-tower Juan and Hernando looked forth upon a sight that might well indeed have caused their courage to fail, their hearts to sink. The throng of Peruvians had grown to be a multitude. The plains, the valleys, the hill tops — all seemed covered with them ; and through the mountain passes, up from the river they surged like a coming wave. Their wild shouts, their shrill war cries, their deafening clang of music struck terror to the brave hearts of the little band of Spaniards.

What was to be done? To attack this numberless foe was worse than useless. To attempt conciliation, enraged as they were at last, was childishness. There seemed nothing to do but to wait, wait, wait. Pizarro might come. Forces might be raised.

But the Peruvians had not come to wait. A long be-seiging of the city was not their policy. Aroused at last, they came to fight, to kill, to destroy, to revenge them-selves, and that, too, *at once*, and with all the speed and cruelty of an infuriated nation. They attacked the city with wild fury. Over the walls, into the city, showers, aye, torrents of arrows, stones, spears poured down upon the Spaniards. Then came great masses of red-hot stones and blazing masses of burning wood. The city was fired ! Up and down the streets and across the buildings the fire spread. From tower to tower leaped the flames, and down, crash on crash, came the great masses of stone and clay. Soon Cuzco was little more than a blazing, smouldering ruin.

And now the angry troops set upon the fortress. A hot,
badly fight with the little band of Spaniards, and it was in
their possession. Now, driven from their stronghold, surrounded on every hand by fire and flame, pressed upon by
the oncoming enemy, Hernando called, " Again to the fortress ! On to the fortress ! Together now, all together,
rush upon the fortress ! It is our only hope ! If die we
must, then there as well as anywhere. On to the fortress !
On ! On ! On to the fortress ! "

For a second the Spaniards quailed. Then Juan sprang
forward. "It can be done, and I will lead the force."
Setting forth from the city, the little band suddenly and to
the utter surprise of the Peruvians fell upon the fortress.
With the desperation of hunted men they assailed it. The
fight was long and terrible. Juan, fighting with the strength
of a giant, pushed his way to the very parapet. The fortress again was theirs. Again the Spanish dash and daring
had conquered the strength and numbers of the Peruvian
troops.

But though the Peruvians drew away, and quiet seemed
to prevail, the Spaniards knew all too well that their suffer-
ings had perhaps but just begun. Their position was inse-

cure.   Pizarro, far from coming to their aid, was himself
in fierce battle ; the whole country was in arms ; the Peruvian spirit, was aroused and Vengeance rode forth upon the
wind.

For five long months Manco besieged the little fortress.
Starvation or death at the hands of the foe seemed the
Spaniards' only choice.   Still they held on.   Pizarro sent
to Panama for aid, begging the governor to send troops
and save the wealth and honor of the Spanish power in
Peru.

At last the Peruvian forces drew away.   Their very
numbers proved their ruin.   Provisions gave out, and
Manco saw too plainly that large numbers of his soldiers
must be sent home to till the fields.

Quickly Hernando divined their situation.   " Now is our
time," said he.   And boldly he sallied forth, attacked the
Peruvians, mowing them down like grain before the scythe.

" We must do more even than this ; we must capture
Manco.   Secure, as he seems to be, in yonder fortress,
on an almost inaccessible cliff, surrounded by his bravest
warriors — still I say he must be recaptured.   There is no
safety for us with him among his people."

It was a perilous expedition. It could not but fail, and yet the desperate Hernando dared try. Early one morning, he, with eighty chosen followers, scaled the steep cliff and attacked the fort. Down came a tempest of rocks and arrows and fiery darts. The Spaniards fought bravely, but defeat was certain; and in a few hours Hernando led the fragment of his little band back into the city. Had they succeeded, Peru would, perhaps, have been theirs once more.

ALMAGRO'S OPPORTUNITY.

Almagro had started southward with his soldiers to find another golden country of which, according to the king's grant, he could take possession for his own governing. But on the journey he had met with nothing but hostility from the natives, starvation and bitter cold.

It was through dreary and desolate wilds they had wandered. And when at last they were reduced to feeding upon the dead horses as their only food, and their hands and feet were frozen in the terrible cold, Almagro turned again northward. The expedition was indeed a terrible failure; .and Almagro, who at his setting forth, had carried with him no little sullen hate towards Pizarro, returned more embittered, and filled more than ever with a sense of his own defeat and unfair treatment.

It was with a grim delight then that, as he neared Cuzco, he heard of the uprising of the people and the siege of the city. To him this seemed a golden opportunity for his own aggrandizement.

His brave little band eagerly listened to his plan for attacking Hernando, and gladly hurried on to this one last struggle for Almagro's success.

It was a black, stormy night; the rain and hail fell in torrents, when Almagro burst into the city, took possession of the square, burned Hernando's house and took him prisoner.

Worn out with the long siege, weak and sick, Hernando's men were able to make little resistance. Almagro was in possession of Cuzco.

But danger was close at hand. Encamped a few miles outside the city, on their way to Hernando's aid, was a

Spanish force sent by Pizarro from Lima, the new city.

"These must be attacked, and at once," said Almagro. "Surprise is our only method of dealing with them."

And so, with no warning of this new foe, the little detachment from Lima was attacked by Almagro and utterly defeated.

And now Pizarro, who all these weeks had awaited with impatient anxiety the arrival of aid from Panama, was gladdened by the appearance at last of vessels laden with provisions and ammunition, and bearing a goodly army of brave soldiers.

Pizarro was indeed sick of war. He was growing old; and, worn out by ambition, and struggle he longed to live his last years in rest in his beautiful new city. But this was not to be. The conquest of Peru had been his dream by night and his thought by day. He had made that conquest, and now he must reap the harvest of his own sowing. It was a bitter harvest; but we know that he had been selfish and greedy, his methods cruel and heartless.

It was in this mood that Pizarro set forth — weary, but full still of firm resolve, his dauntless determination not one whit lessened.

Hardly had he left the valley when there reached him news of Almagro's revolt and the capture of Hernando. Moreover, a detachment sent forward had been routed by Almagro, who was advancing to meet him.

"We must return and receive our coming guests within our new city," said Pizarro with grim humor. A messenger was sent to meet Almagro and offer terms of agreement. But it was too late now. Almagro, who would once have been satisfied with half the power, now, flushed with success, scorned any terms and demanded all. "Cuzco is mine — and Hernando," said he. "And Lima *shall* be mine — and, perhaps, Pizarro."

It was not long before these two, once such friends and help-meets, met in the valley with their forces. It would have been as well, perhaps, had they engaged in battle, and so have settled the dispute for supremacy. Instead, however, after some little quarrelling and bickering, a sort of compromise was made, Hernando was freed, and Pizarro in return solemnly promised to await honestly the decision of the king in the matter of Cuzco.

But Pizarro had little regard for his promises. No sooner was Hernando freed, than Pizarro sent word to Almagro that he would not abide by the treaty made the day before, but should proceed in whatever way seemed to him best.

Almagro, on hearing this, broke camp, and speedily retreated to Cuzco. "We must not meet in battle here," said he, " but we will die, if need be, in defending Cuzco, the city that belongs to us."

THE BATTLE.

Hardly had Almagro reached the city, than across the plain came Pizarro's army, headed by Hernando.

Almagro himself, sick and unable to raise himself, was carried to his watch tower, while his army, under his faithful officer Orgonez, went forth to meet Hernando.

Orgonez took his stand and awaited the approach of the foe.   On the hill tops swarms of Peruvians watched with savage delight the white men arrayed against each other.

Hard and hot the battle raged.   The two leaders, always bitter enemies, now closed in deadly combat.   Orgonez fell.   The foe gathered around him.

"I wish honorably to surrender," said Orgonez, proudly. "Is there a knight here who will receive my sword?" A cowardly soldier sprang forward, took the sword, and then, dastard that he was, plunged a dagger into the brave cavalier's heart.

A shout of rage arose from Orgonez's troops.

"Vengeance! vengeance!" shouted Lerma, another officer. And rushing into the midst of the foe he sought out Hernando and fell upon him in desperate fury. Hernando and Lerma, charging upon each other, both fell wounded. Now the tide of battle swept in between them, and they were parted. A little longer the battle raged, then Almagro's troops turned and fled. Hernando hotly pursued, and seizing upon Almagro himself, who was being carried on a litter by his faithful servants, threw him into prison, and entered the city triumphant. Again Hernando held Cuzco, and Almagro was his captive.

"When I was his prisoner, he was kind to me, he spared me, he saved me when his officers would have had me put to death, and he freed me," Hernando said to himself many times a day, as he thought of what must be Almagro's fate. "And still I dare not let him live. I have promised him that he should be spared, but it cannot be. Almagro must die."

The sick old man, his mind at rest in Hernando's promises, lay dying in his cell. Suddenly, one day, his door was thrown open, two soldiers entered and roughly seizing him, dragged him forth to trial.

"You are to be tried for treason!" said they. The trial, like those of Atahualpa and the old chief, was a mere form. Almagro was already doomed. As his death sentence reached his ears, Almagro, who, whatever had been his faults, was now merely a sick and dying man, and so might well have been spared this cruelty, fell upon his knees at Hernando's feet. "O spare me this cruel death," begged he. "What harm can I do you in the few days there would be left me to live? Look at me; does this weak, sick body look like a dangerous foe to you? Think you my spirit is not already broken, and that I would, if I could, arouse one enemy against you? Spare me! spare me to die peacefully in my cell!"

But Hernando was hardened. "Arise," said he, with a sneer; "shame upon you, that you grovel like a dog." And with these words he turned and left him.

The next day, a priest and a hangman entered Almagro's cell.   The priest prayed with him ; the hangman strangled him.   Such was the cruelty and wickedness of the times.

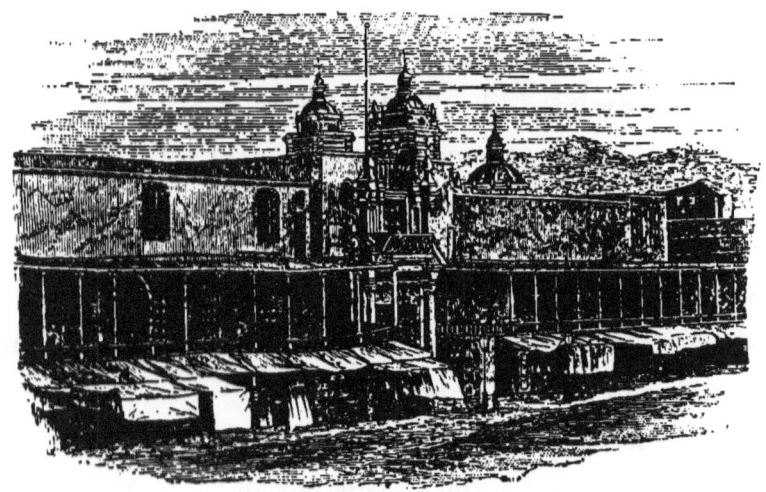

FRONT OF PIZARRO'S PALACE.

PLOT AGAINST PIZARRO.

The death of Almagro was not long to be unavenged. Almagro had left a son who, unfortunately for Pizarro,

had inherited all his father's fire and ambition, and his re-
vengeful spirit, perhaps, as well.

This son, Diego, was living in Lima, in a large, beautiful building in the square in which Pizarro lived. He had
great wealth, and lived a gay, reckless life among his companions.

There were in this city many of Almagro's old friends,
who, now that the old cavalier was dead, devoted themselves to adhering closely to Diego and heartily hating Pizarro.

Pizarro was now in Lima again, busy with his plans for
the city, and resting in, what seemed to him, perfect secu-
rity. Surely the Peruvian troops would hardly be likely
to combine again after such disasters under their leader:
Panama was friendly; the king was full of approval; and
there seemed now nothing to interfere with Pizarro's selfish ambition to be himself "head and front" of all Peru.

But all this time that he had been away from Lima at-
tending to the affairs of war, Diego and his friends had
been secretly at work. Night after night they met together,
to drink and carouse, to rehearse their wrongs, and to
plan revenge upon Pizarro.

Pizarro had been warned that, such meetings were being held; but he, too proud to admit that fear of Almagro's son could for a moment be entertained by him, pretended indifference and scorn whenever he was told of them.

"Miserable wretches," he would say, "what can they do to me? Let them go their way. They have hardship enough." And so they were left free to meet and conspire as they pleased. Whenever they came in his way, Pizarro treated them with contempt, pretending not to know of their presence even. All this added to their hatred, and when Pizarro's secretary, a pompous, strutting man, began also to insult them, the conspirators grew more and more bitter, more and more determined to be done with this hateful tyrant, as they called their governor.

One dark, stormy night, twenty of Almagro's most loyal followers met at young Diego's house. Very stealthily they entered and were conducted to a secluded room in the back of the building. Diego received them quietly, and they took their places around a large table. By Diego's side sat a dark, fierce-looking Spaniard, with shining black hair, and wicked, glittering eyes.

The room was only feebly lighted, and the Spaniards were all closely muffled in long black cloaks. The fierce-looking man began to talk in a low, earnest tone with Diego. Diego looked startled, but the glittering eyes were fixed upon him, and the speaker went on, gesticulating fiercely and earnestly, frequently appealing to his companions, until at last Diego, and all, seemed to agree upon some plan to murder Pizarro.

The plan that this Spanish cavalier revealed to Diego was this: Pizarro, on the following Sunday as he returned from the cathedral to his home, should be suddenly attacked by this band of men and stabbed.

There was, however, one of the men who, for some reason of his own, objected to this plot, and secretly resolved that it should never be carried out. So, turning against his own fellow conspirators, with that ready lack of honor so common to these people, he went at once to the priest and revealed the whole plot. The priest, in alarm, hastened to Pizarro's house and told the whole story.

"Oh! ha! ha!" laughed Pizarro, loudly. "You are a very cunning priest. You see in this a way to higher honors. But fear not for me. Pizarro has faced a foe

more times than once.   Do you think to frighten him with
such a story now?"

The priest went away, crestfallen and frightened.   Pizarro, for all his loud bragging and insolent laughing, thought
it well to inform the judge of the plot, and to remain safely
in his house on Sunday.

Death of Pizarro.

Early on the morning of that day, the conspirators met
at Diego's house, which chanced to stand beside the cathedral.   The windows on the cathedral side were heavily cur-
tained, and from these the men eagerly watched the arrival
of the people at church.

"He has not come, or have we missed him?" said they
when all had entered.

"He comes always with a guard of soldiers, — we could
not have missed him!" said one.

"He may have come alone.   Let us wait until mass is
over, and he comes out from church," said another.

And so the murderers waited. At last the people came
forth. The cathedral was deserted, but no Pizarro had
appeared.

The men stared at each other. " Can it be our plot was
discovered?" said the fierce-looking leader. "If so, we
may as well — "

" Flee the city! Flee the city!" interrupted one of the
conspirators.

"Flee the city?" cried the leader. "Never, till that
tyrant, that murderer of Almagro lies soaked in his own
blood! Flee the city! Cowards! Rather let us strike
the tyrant down! Let us to his house! Follow me!"
And with these words he rushed forth into the square
shouting, " Death to the tyrant! Death, death to the
tyrant!"

The men followed, others joined the party, and together
they rushed to Pizarro's house. In through the courtyard,
through the door, up the great staircase, straight to Pizarro's room rushed the excited band.

Pizarro's servants were now up in arms; and, rushing upon the conspirators, a fierce hand-to-hand struggle
followed. Pizarro, hearing the commotion, boldly stepped

DEATH OF PIZARRO.

into the midst of the combat.   Before the conspirators even
knew of his presence, he was dealing deadly blows on every
side.   Like a tiger he fought, and, old as he was, he drove
back his assailants with his fierce blows.   " Vile traitors ! "
cried he, as they fell stricken to the earth by his sweeping
sabre, " Do you think to murder me in my own house?
Down with you !   Down with you ! "

For a moment his assailants were stunned,   About him
lay already many of the conspirators writhing in the agony
of death.

"Upon him !   Upon him !   Cowards, all of us !   We are
here to kill the tyrant !   The tyrant !   The tyrant !" cried
the leader, gathering himself for a fresh attack.   At this
they closed around Pizarro, and five swords were plunged
into his body.   With a groan he fell, the blood spurting
from his wounds.   One more plunge of the swords, and
with a shudder Pizarro sank, dead.

"The tyrant is dead !   The tyrant is dead !   Diego is
governor !   Diego is governor !" shouted the half-wild murderers, rushing out upon the street again.   " Our laws are
restored !   The tyrant is dead !   Long live Diego !   Long
live Diego ! "

The city was soon in the wildest excitement. Pizarro's house was plundered, his secretary was cast into prison, and but for the stern refusal and the protection of Diego, his body would have been dragged into the square, and hanged.

" There is nothing to be gained," said he, " by mutilating Pizarro's dead body. I command that it be spared all insult."

And so the body was quietly taken into the cathedral and a hurried midnight funeral mass said over it.

It was years after, when the body was taken from its resting place and placed in a magnificent tomb near the high altar. Later still, when Lima's new cathedral was built, it was again removed, and entombed, with all the honors of the country.

Pizarro was a wonderful man — one of the greatest in history ; one of Spain's noblest subjects, and bravest, most enduring, most persevering soldiers. Judge each for yourself wherein his grandeur lay, and remember it. Judge each for yourself wherein his faults and vices lay ; avoid, and then forget them.

APPENDIX.

SONGS OF WAR.

The Soldier's Funeral.

The muffled drum rolled on the air,
Warriors with stately step were there ;
On every arm was the black crape bound.
Every carbine was turned to the ground ;
Solemn the sound of their measured tread,
As silent and slow they followed the dead.
The riderless horse was led in the rear,
There were white plumes waving over the bier,
Helmet and sword were laid on the pall,

125

For it was a soldier's funeral.
That soldier had stood on the battle plain
Where every step was over the slain,
But the brand and the ball had passed him by,
And he came to his native land — to die!
'Twas hard to come to that native land,
And not clasp one familiar hand!
'Twas hard to be numbered amid the dead,
Or ere he could hear his welcome said!
But 'twas something to see its cliffs once more
And to lay his bones on his own loved shore;
To think that the friends of his youth might weep
O'er the green grass turf of the soldier's sleep.
The bugles ceased their wailing sound
As the coffin was lowered into the ground;
A volley was fired, a blessing said,
One moment's pause — and they left the dead! —
I saw a poor and aged man,
His step was feeble, his lip was wan;
He knelt him down on the new-raised mound,
His face was bowed to the cold damp ground;
He raised his head, his tears were done,
The FATHER had prayed o'er his only son.

— MRS MCLEAN.

Soldier, Rest!

Soldier, rest! thy warfare o'er,
   Sleep the sleep that knows not breaking;
Dream of battle fields no more,
   Days of danger, nights of waking.
In our isles enchanted hall,
   Hands unseen thy couch are strewing;
Fairy strains of music fall,
   Every sense in slumber dewing.
Soldier, rest! thy warfare o'er,
Dream of fighting fields no more;
Sleep the sleep that knows not breaking,
Morn of toil, nor night of waking.

         — WALTER SCOTT — *Song from " The Lady of the Lake."*

Fife and Drum.

The trumpet's loud clangor
Excites us to arms,